Sylvie's Seahorse

MARA BERGMAN

ILLUSTRATED BY

TOR FREEMAN

For my mother
M. B.

For Dad
T. F.

First published 2006 by Walker Books Ltd
87 Vauxhall Walk, London SE11 5HJ

2 4 6 8 10 9 7 5 3 1

Text © 2006 Mara Bergman
Illustrations © 2006 Tor Freeman

The right of Mara Bergman and Tor Freeman to be identified as
author and illustrator respectively of this work has been asserted by them
in accordance with the Copyright, Designs and Patents Act 1988

This book has been typeset in Bembo Educational

Printed and bound in Great Britain by
Creative Print and Design (Wales), Ebbw Vale

British Library Cataloguing in Publication Data:
a catalogue record for this book is available from the British Library

ISBN-13: 978-1-4063-0194-6
ISBN-10: 1-4063-0194-9

www.walkerbooks.co.uk

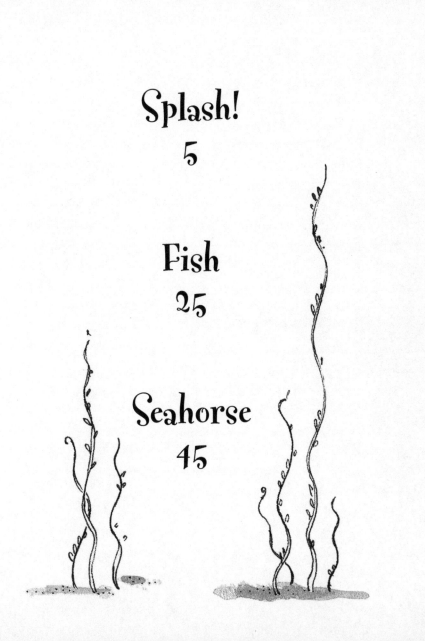

Splash!

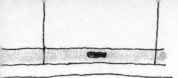

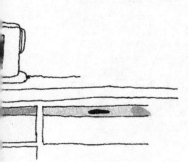

It was Saturday, and Saturday was swim day.

"Can we go soon?" asked Sylvie at breakfast.

"Yes," said Mum, "but first we must feed Joy's cats."

Joy lived next door. Whenever she
went on holiday, Sylvie and Mum
looked after her cats. Joy was away
now, visiting her sister in Jamaica.

Sylvie liked going to
Joy's house. As soon
as she and Mum and
Jamie arrived, the
cats ran straight up
to her.

8

"Miaow, miaow!" they said as they rubbed against her legs.

"Hello, Shirley and Graham," said Sylvie. "Hello, Gypsy."

Mum unlocked the back door, and
Sylvie took a tin of cat food from the
fridge. She scooped out the food onto
three plates and put them outside,
on the step. The cats gobbled it up.

Walking home
afterwards, Mum said,
"You are such a big
help, Sylvie."

"So can we
go now?" Sylvie
asked. She liked
being a big help,
but she liked
going to the
pool even more.

Mum was teaching her to swim.

"Of course," said Mum, and soon
they were on their way.

When they arrived at the sports centre, Mum and Sylvie took Jamie to the crèche. There were lots of other babies there too.

Then they went
to the changing
room. There were
rows and rows
of lockers. After
changing into their
swimsuits, they
piled their clothes
into one of them.

Mum gave Sylvie a pound coin and
Sylvie pushed it through the slot.
She shut the door and gave
the key to Mum.
Mum wore it
around her ankle.

The pool was huge and
blue and friendly. Lots
of people were in it
already, swimming
and splashing
and playing.

Sylvie and Mum went down the steps
into the shallow end.

They pretended they were mermaids.
Then Mum turned into a crocodile
and chased Sylvie, calling,
"I'm going to get you!"

After a while,
Mum said,
"Time to do
some proper
swimming
now. Let's
see how far
my little fish
can swim today."

Sylvie liked it
when Mum called her a fish.

Mum held Sylvie around the waist
and started walking. Sylvie pulled her
arms through the water and kicked
her feet. Then Mum let go.

Sylvie's feet
sank straight to
the bottom.
"Let's try again,"
said Mum.

But again it didn't work.
"Let's try the other
way," said Sylvie.

Sylvie went to the side of the pool and Mum stood in front of her. Sylvie stretched out her arms and kicked her legs. Mum caught her.

"Good," said Mum. "Let's do that again."

But this time when Sylvie kicked off, there was a huge SPLASH! as one of the big children jumped into the pool.

SPLASH!

Sylvie went under the water.
Water got into her mouth
and ears and nose.

Mum rushed over
as Sylvie came up again.
She was spluttering
and coughing.

19

Then a lifeguard
came over. "Are you
OK?" she asked.

Sylvie didn't look very happy,
but she nodded anyway.

"She just had a little
scare," said Mum.
"Thank you."

Then, "Shall we
have another go,
Sylvie?"

But Sylvie didn't want to. She had
had enough swimming for one day.

As they got dressed, Mum said, "Let's
get Jamie and go to the café. I think
we could do with a treat."

Jamie was happy to see Sylvie and
Mum, and he loved going to the café.
While Sylvie ate her muffin and
drank her apple juice she watched
the swimmers.

Some were bigger than Sylvie
and some were smaller than Jamie.
Some were standing and some were
swimming. Some were splashing too.

Sylvie's swimming hadn't gone all that well today, but she would try again.
She would try and try and try. Sylvie knew that one day she would do it. She would swim – just like a fish.

Fish

Every morning that week, Sylvie
and Jamie and Mum fed Joy's cats. On
Saturday, when they got back home,
the phone rang.

"It's Uncle Jack," said Mum. "He's
taking Matt to see the fish at the
aquarium. Would you like to go along,
Sylvie?"

"Yes!" Sylvie shouted. She liked fish.

"It means missing our swim," said Mum. "Just for today, though. What do you think?"

Sylvie thought about last time, when a big splash had stopped her from swimming.

She still wanted to learn to swim, but she liked the idea of doing something else today, especially with her cousin and uncle.

"I'd like to go with Uncle Jack and Matty," she said.

"Good," said Mum. Then, speaking into the phone again she said, "She'd love to go, Jack. See you soon."

It wasn't long
before Uncle
Jack called out,
"Anybody home?"

He always said
that when he came over.
"We're going to see sharks, we're
going to see sharks!" said Matt. He
was excited.

"Have a lovely time," said Mum. "Be good!" She and Jamie waved goodbye from the door.

31

At the aquarium, Sylvie and Matt and Uncle Jack bought tickets from the desk. Then they went through a turnstile.

Sylvie couldn't believe how many tanks of fish there were!

More than anything, Matt wanted to look at the sharks, so they went straight there. They watched them for a *l-o-n-g* time.

Finally, Uncle Jack said, "I don't know about anyone else, but I'd like to see some other fish."

And they did!

They saw fish with stripes and fish with spots,

 colourful fish darting in huge tanks and horseshoe crabs they could touch.

They came to a room with smaller
tanks. In the first one were creatures that
looked exactly like horses – or at least
their heads looked like horses' heads.

36

Their bodies curved round and ended
in long tails that curled forwards.

"Aren't they amazing!"
said Uncle Jack.

"What are they?"
asked Sylvie.

"They're seahorses,"
said Uncle Jack.

"Seahorses
are a very
special type of fish.
See the way some of
them are holding onto
the plants? They're also
the slowest swimmers
in the world."

The seahorses were like nothing Sylvie had ever seen. They were different colours – blue and red and green and brown. Their eyes kept moving, and the seahorses seemed to drift instead of swim.

"They have a breeding programme here," explained Uncle Jack after reading the sign on the wall. "Some seahorses are endangered, and the aquarium helps to protect them."

In the next tank was a seahorse with a very large tummy. It was rocking back and forth, back and forth. Tiny bubbles began to drift upwards.

"What are those bubbles?" Matt asked.

"I don't think they're bubbles," said
Uncle Jack. "Look very, very closely."

Sylvie and Matt did. Uncle Jack was
right, they weren't bubbles at all. They
were seahorses – and there seemed
to be hundreds of them!
Each tiny perfect seahorse
was no larger than
a comma in a book.
After shooting
out from the big
seahorse's tummy,
they slowly
drifted to the top
of the tank.

41

"Aren't they sweet!" said Sylvie. "What a lucky mummy to have so many babies!"

Uncle Jack laughed. "Actually, that's the daddy – the daddy seahorses have the babies."

Sylvie could have watched for ever.

"It's getting
crowded now,"
said Uncle Jack.
"It's time this
daddy got his
little seahorses
home!"

"Goodbye,"
Sylvie whispered.

All the way home and for the
rest of the day, Sylvie
thought about
the seahorses.
That night she
even dreamed
about them.

In her dream,
Sylvie was
swimming – Sylvie
was swimming
with seahorses.

Seahorse

The next Saturday was cold and wet.
Mum said, "This is the last time we will
need to feed Joy's cats."

"For ever?" Sylvie asked.

"No," said Mum. "Just for now. Joy
is coming home today."

The cats came running up to Sylvie
like they always did. She put their
food on the plates and
put the plates
out the back.
Mum wrote
a note for Joy:

Saturday

WELCOME HOME, JOY!

Hope you had a
great time.
We fed the cats
at 8.30.
See you later!

Naomi, Sylvie + Jamie
xx

When they got home, Mum said,
"Let's get ready for swimming."

Sylvie had almost forgotten
about swimming. It seemed
such a long time since
they last went.

"Can Jamie come in
the pool too?" asked Sylvie.

"He'd love that," said Mum.

49

Sylvie was glad
there weren't many
people in the pool.
She didn't want
to get splashed
like last time.

She and Jamie
and Mum played
Ring-a-ring o'roses.
Jamie laughed.

They played
Humpty Dumpty.
Jamie laughed
and laughed.

They played Motor Boat, Motor
Boat, and that was the best of all.
Jamie didn't even
notice when
his face got
splashed.

"OK, young man," said Mum. Sylvie liked it when Mum called Jamie a young man. "You're having a rest now."

Mum put Jamie into one of the playpens by the poolside. Straight away he started playing with a dolphin.

"Now, my little fish," Mum said
to Sylvie, "let's see you swim.
Remember, take it
nice and slowly."

A few more people were in the pool
now, but Sylvie was feeling brave.
She went to the side and stretched
out her arms. She kicked off with
her feet. Mum caught her.

"Again!" said Sylvie.

This time, Mum stood back quite a
bit when Sylvie kicked off. But Sylvie
sank before she reached her.

Mum rushed over just as Sylvie popped
out of the water. But Sylvie was smiling.
"I remembered to hold
my breath," she said.
"*And* I shut my eyes."
"Good," said Mum.
"Let's have
another go."

Sylvie pushed off the side of the pool again. She wanted to swim so badly! She remembered all the fish she had seen swimming at the aquarium, especially the seahorses. They may be the slowest swimmers in the world, but even the tiniest ones could swim as soon as they were born.

Sylvie kicked and stretched out
her arms. She cupped her hands and
brought them down into the water.
There was so much to think about!

She remembered to keep kicking and
moving her arms. She would do it, she
would do it, she—

"You've done it!" said Mum.

And she had! Sylvie had gone all the way across the pool.

"You *are* a fish!" said Mum, hugging her. "My very special fish."

Just as they arrived back home, Joy came over.

"Hi!" she called. "Thanks so much for looking after the cats."

"Any time," said Mum. "We enjoyed it."

Sylvie couldn't wait to tell Joy her news.

"I swam all the way across the pool today!" she said.

"That's wonderful, Sylvie," said Joy. "Well done! Then I've really got the perfect present for you."

Joy handed Sylvie a very small parcel, and there was one for Mum too. She gave a larger one to Jamie.

Slowly, Sylvie opened
her parcel and found …
a seahorse! It was silver
and its tail could move.
Sylvie could hardly believe it.

"It's amazing!"
she said.

"Seahorses are
amazing!" said Joy.

"I saw some in
the sea when I went
swimming near where
my sister lives."

As Sylvie held the seahorse, she pictured Joy swimming with seahorses. Then she thought of her visit to the aquarium with Uncle Jack and Matty, and all the baby seahorses. They *were* amazing.

Then Sylvie thought about learning to swim – and that was amazing too.